THE ALL NEW! BATMAN
THE BRAVE AND THE BOLD

STONE ARCH BOOKS
a capstone imprint

STONE ARCH BOOKS™

Published in 2015 by Stone Arch Books
A Capstone Imprint
1710 Roe Crest Drive
North Mankato, MN 56003
www.capstonepub.com

Originally published by DC Comics in the U.S. in single magazine form as The All-New Batman: The Brave and the Bold #6.
Original U.S. Editor: Jim Chadwick

DC Comics
1700 Broadway, New York, NY 10019
A Warner Bros. Entertainment Company

Library of Congress Cataloging-in-Publication Data

Fisch, Sholly, author.
Clobbered by Clayface! / Sholly Fisch, writer ; Rick Burchett, penciller ; Dan Davis, inker ; Gabe Eltaeb, colorist.
pages cm. -- [The all-new Batman: the brave and the bold ; 6]
"Originally published by DC Comics in the U.S. in single magazine form as The All-New Batman: The Brave and the Bold #6."
"Batman created by Bob Kane."
Summary: It is a battle of wits when the Martian Manhunter challenges Batman to penetrate his baffling array of shape-shifting disguises, but when the game goes awry, can the two heroes defeat the most unexpected menace of all?
ISBN 978-1-4342-9663-4 [library binding]
1. Batman [Fictitious character]--Comic books, strips, etc. 2. Batman [Fictitious character]--Juvenile fiction. 3. Superheroes--Comic books, strips, etc. 4. Superheroes--Juvenile fiction. 5. Shapeshifting--Comic books, strips, etc. 6. Shapeshifting--Juvenile fiction. 7. Graphic novels. [1. Graphic novels. 2. Superheroes--Fiction. 3. Shapeshifting--Fiction.] I. Burchett, Rick, illustrator. II. Kane, Bob, creator. III. Title.

PZ7.7.F57Cl 2015
741.5'973--dc23

2014028255

STONE ARCH BOOKS
Ashley C. Andersen Zantop Publisher
Michael Dahl Editorial Director
Eliza Leahy Editor
Heather Kindseth Creative Director
Bob Lentz Art Director
Peggie Carley Designer
Katy LaVigne Production Specialist

Printed in China by Nordica.
0914/CA21401510
092014 008470NORDS15

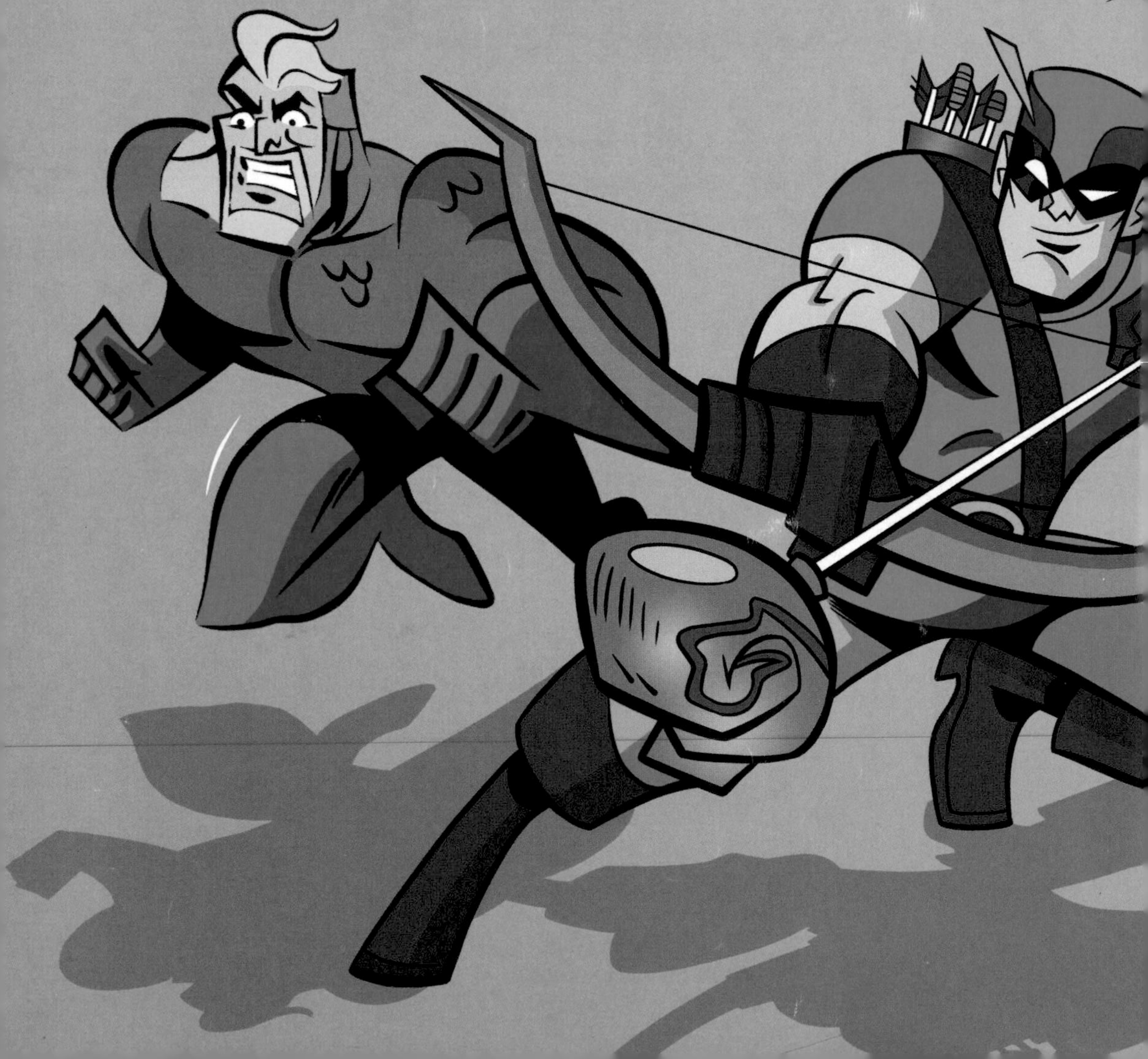

THE ALL NEW!

BATMAN
THE BRAVE AND THE BOLD

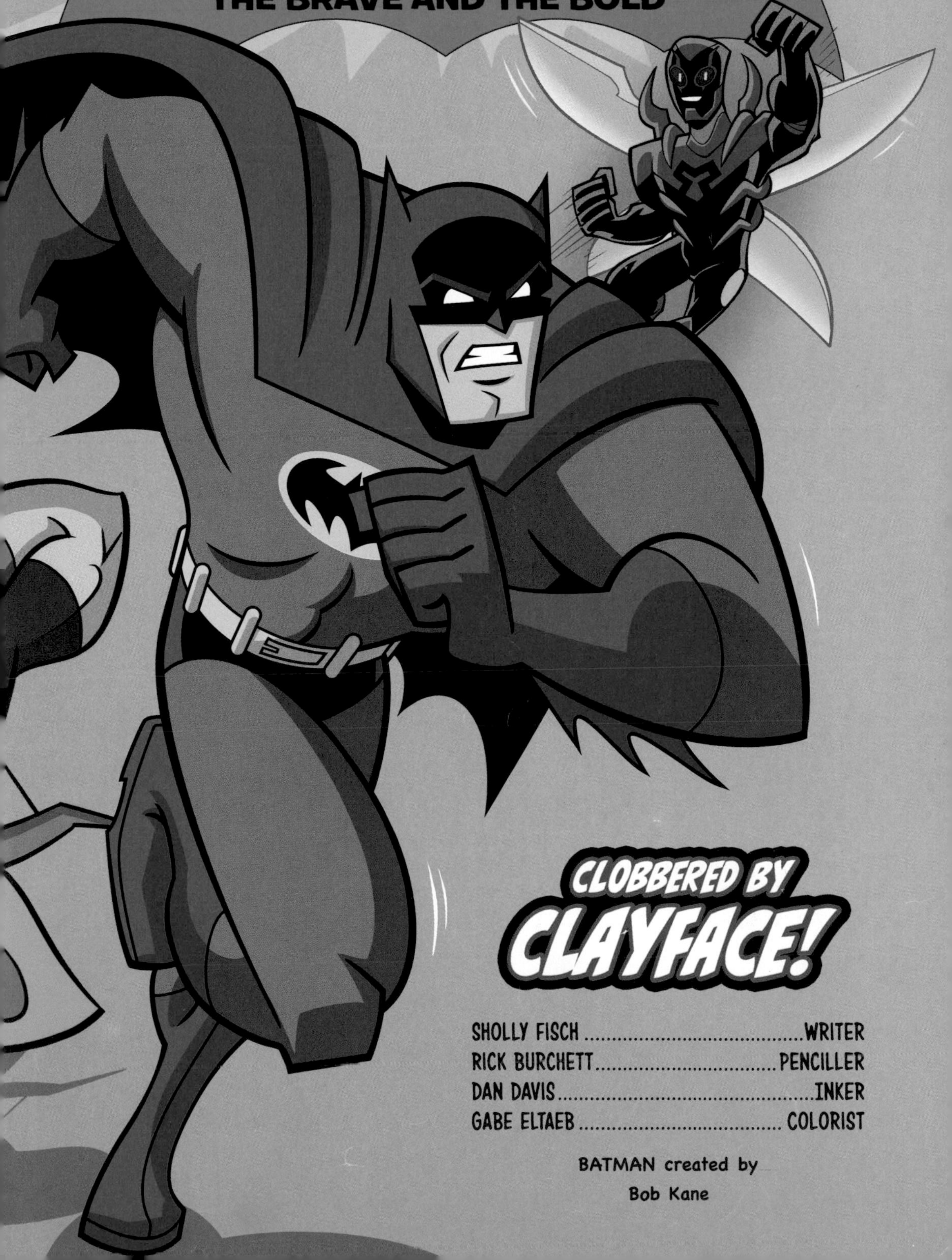

CLOBBERED BY CLAYFACE!

SHOLLY FISCH .... WRITER
RICK BURCHETT................................ PENCILLER
DAN DAVIS.. INKER
GABE ELTAEB .... COLORIST

BATMAN created by
Bob Kane

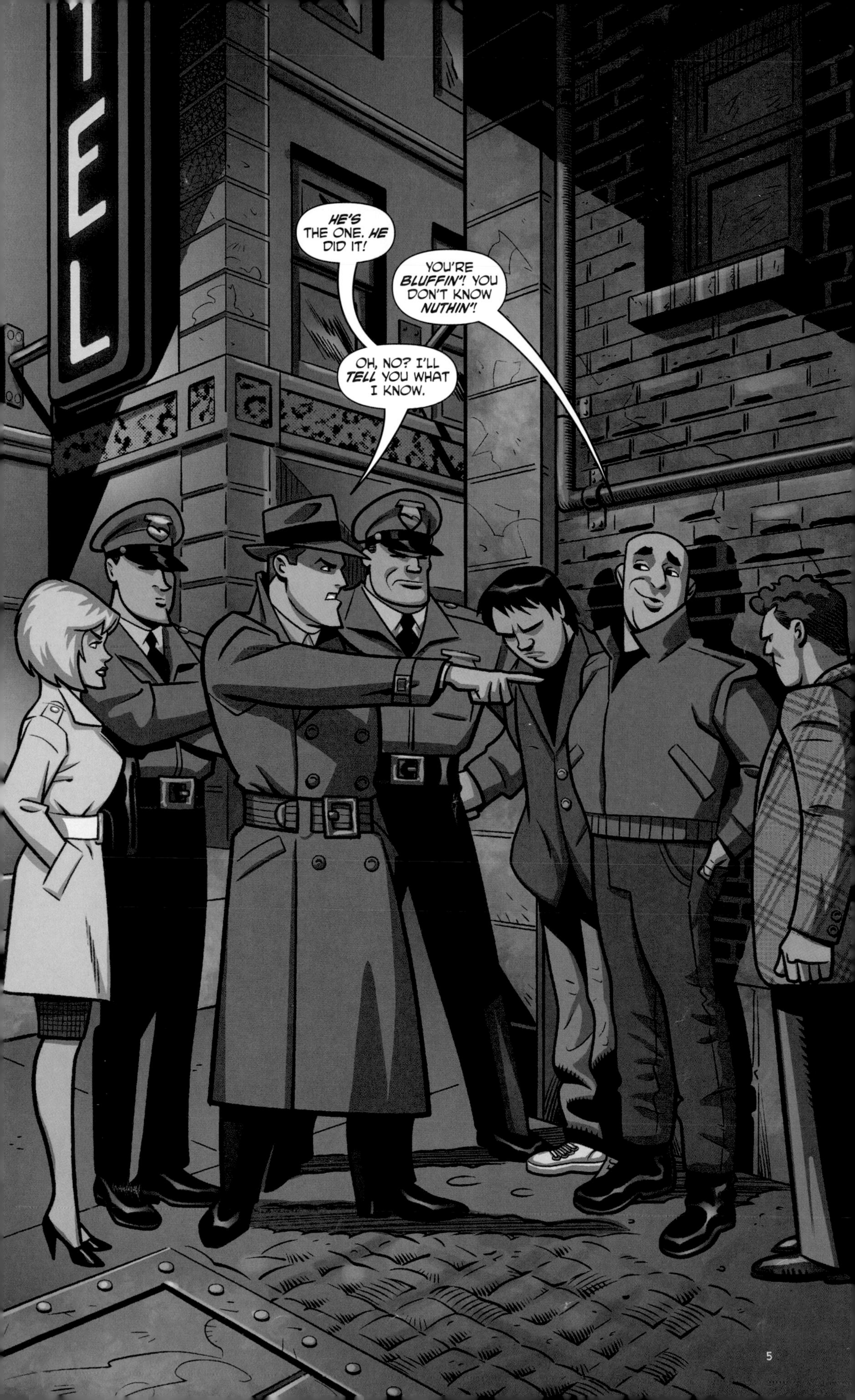
HE'S THE ONE. HE DID IT!
YOU'RE BLUFFIN'! YOU DON'T KNOW NUTHIN'!
OH, NO? I'LL TELL YOU WHAT I KNOW.

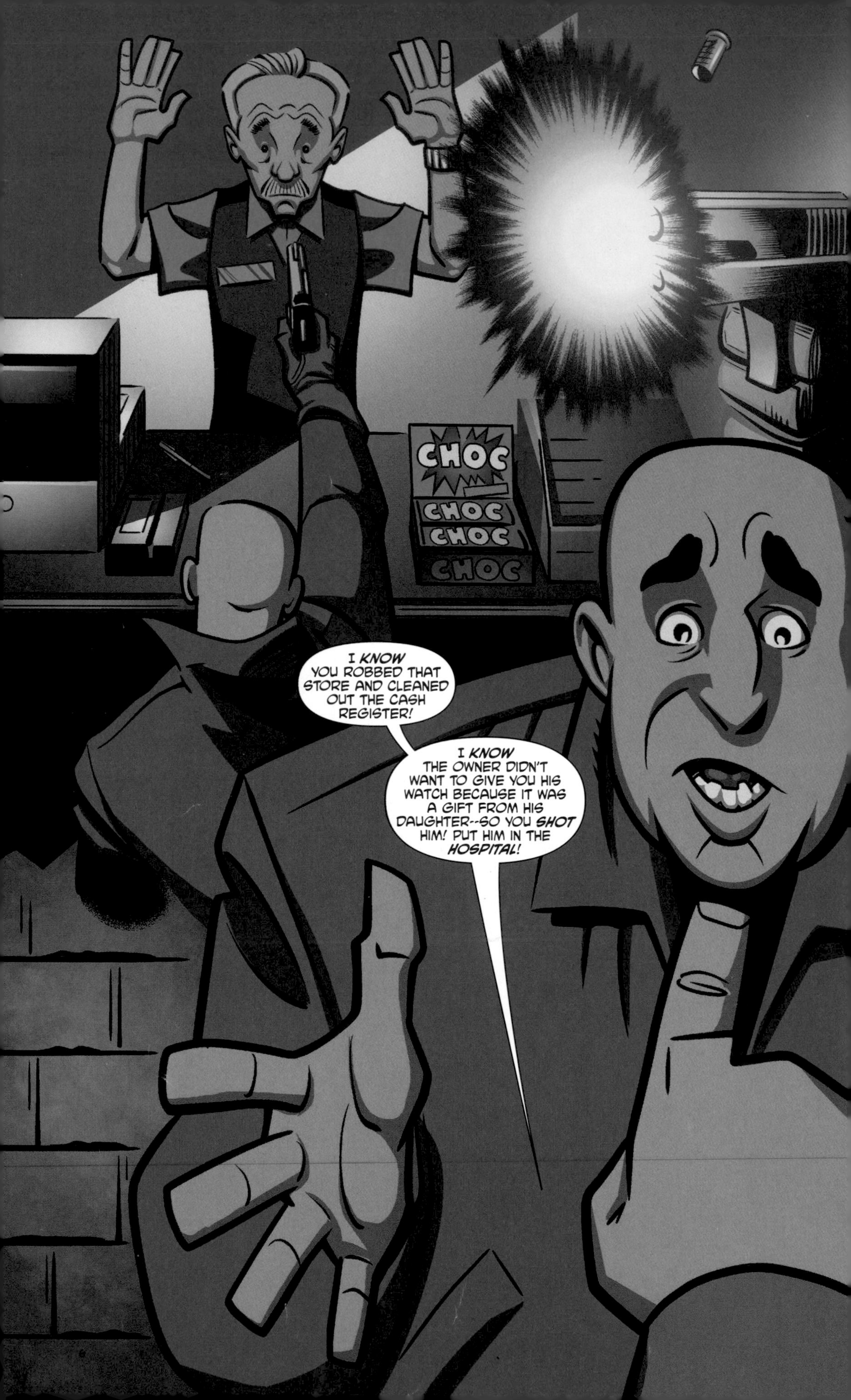
CHOC
CHOC
CHOC
CHOC
I KNOW YOU ROBBED THAT STORE AND CLEANED OUT THE CASH REGISTER!
I KNOW THE OWNER DIDN'T WANT TO GIVE YOU HIS WATCH BECAUSE IT WAS A GIFT FROM HIS DAUGHTER--SO YOU SHOT HIM! PUT HIM IN THE HOSPITAL!

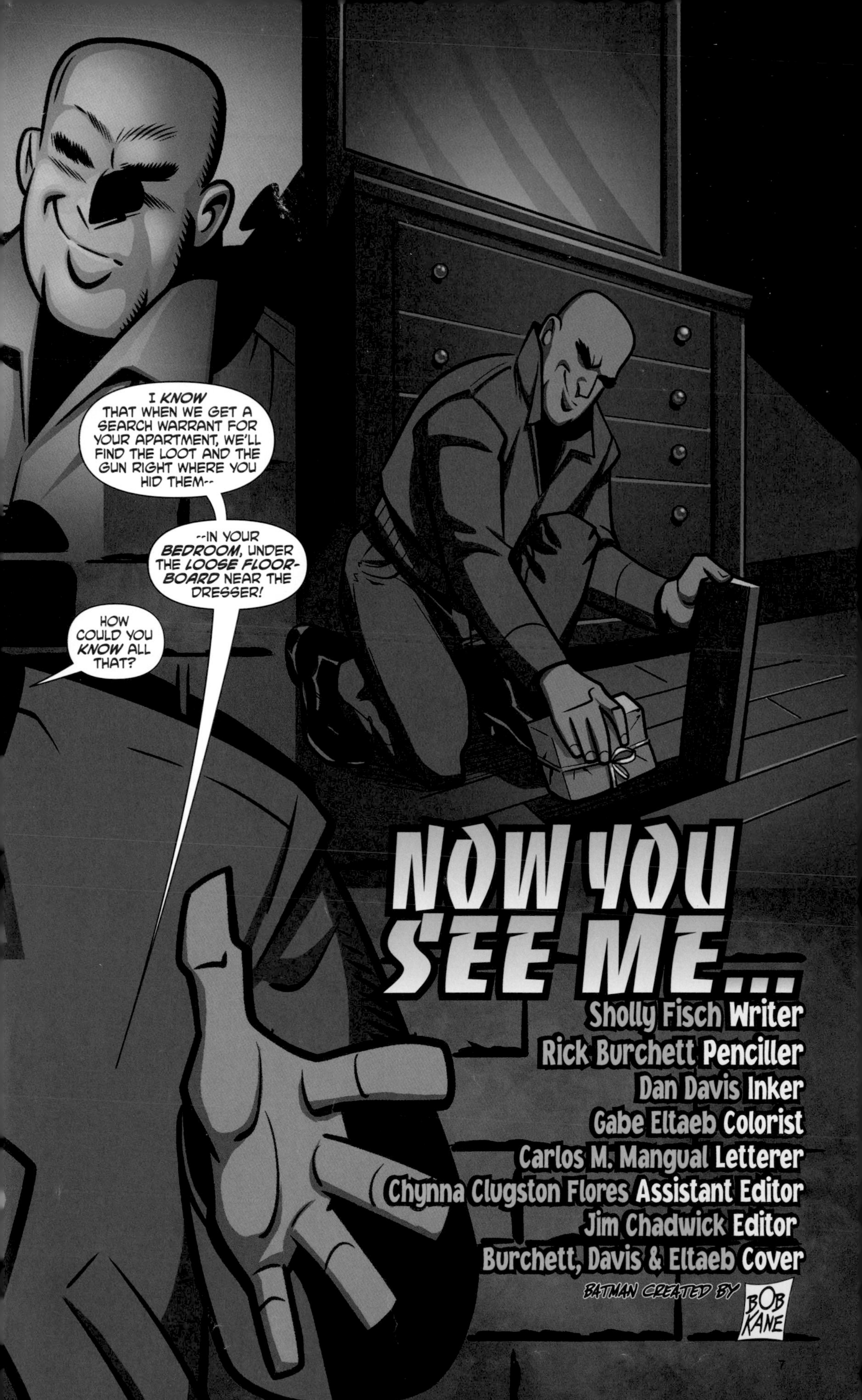
I *KNOW* THAT WHEN WE GET A SEARCH WARRANT FOR YOUR APARTMENT, WE'LL FIND THE LOOT AND THE GUN RIGHT WHERE YOU HID THEM--
--IN YOUR *BEDROOM*, UNDER THE *LOOSE FLOOR-BOARD* NEAR THE DRESSER!
HOW COULD YOU *KNOW* ALL THAT?
NOW YOU SEE ME...
Sholly Fisch Writer
Rick Burchett Penciller
Dan Davis Inker
Gabe Eltaeb Colorist
Carlos M. Mangual Letterer
Chynna Clugston Flores Assistant Editor
Jim Chadwick Editor
Burchett, Davis & Eltaeb Cover
BATMAN CREATED BY BOB KANE

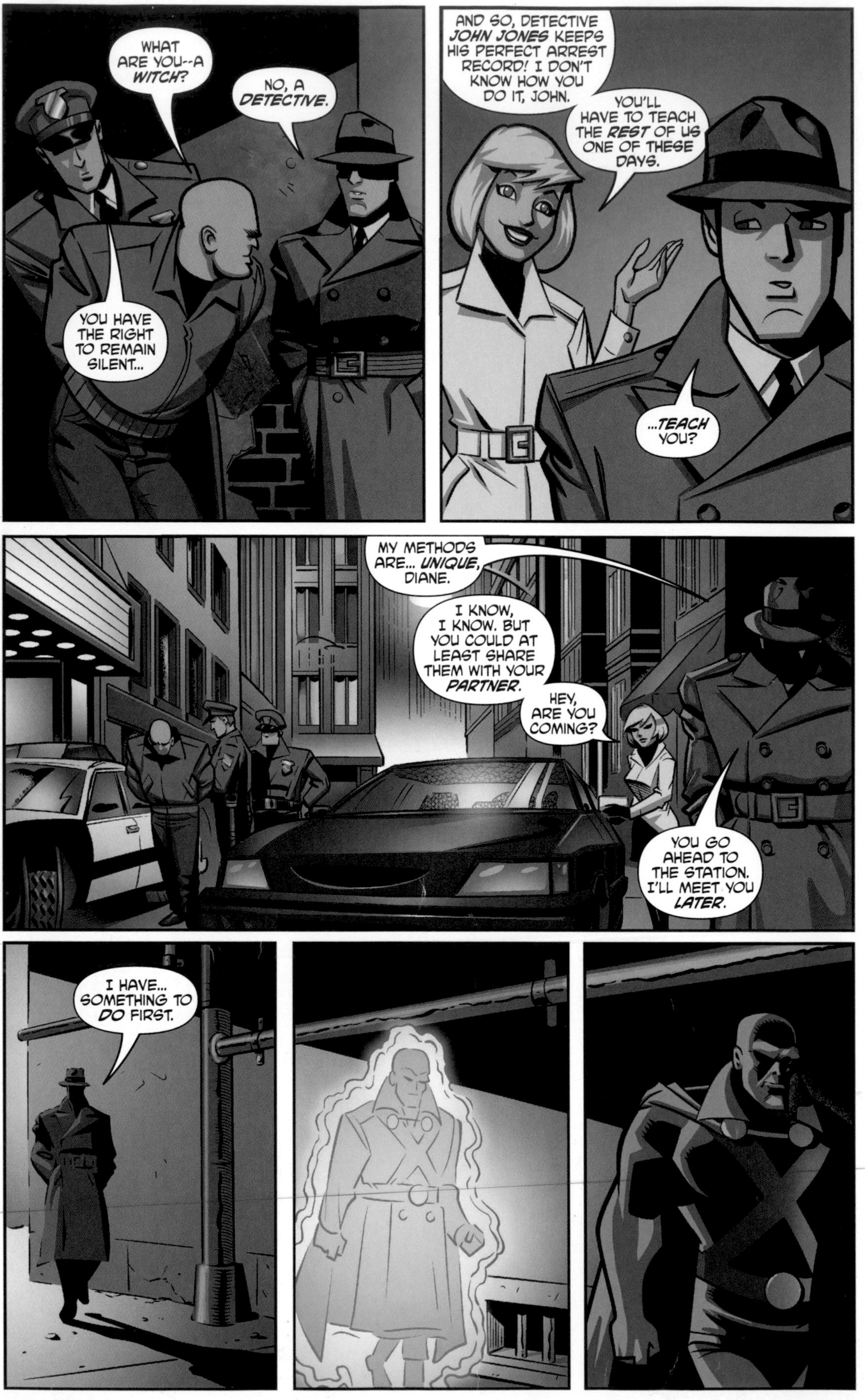
WHAT ARE YOU--A *WITCH*?
NO, A *DETECTIVE*.
YOU HAVE THE RIGHT TO REMAIN SILENT...
AND SO, DETECTIVE *JOHN JONES* KEEPS HIS PERFECT ARREST RECORD! I DON'T KNOW HOW YOU DO IT, JOHN.
YOU'LL HAVE TO TEACH THE *REST* OF US ONE OF THESE DAYS.
...*TEACH* YOU?
MY METHODS ARE... *UNIQUE*, DIANE.
I KNOW, I KNOW. BUT YOU COULD AT LEAST SHARE THEM WITH YOUR *PARTNER*.
HEY, ARE YOU COMING?
YOU GO AHEAD TO THE STATION. I'LL MEET YOU *LATER*.
I HAVE... SOMETHING TO *DO* FIRST.

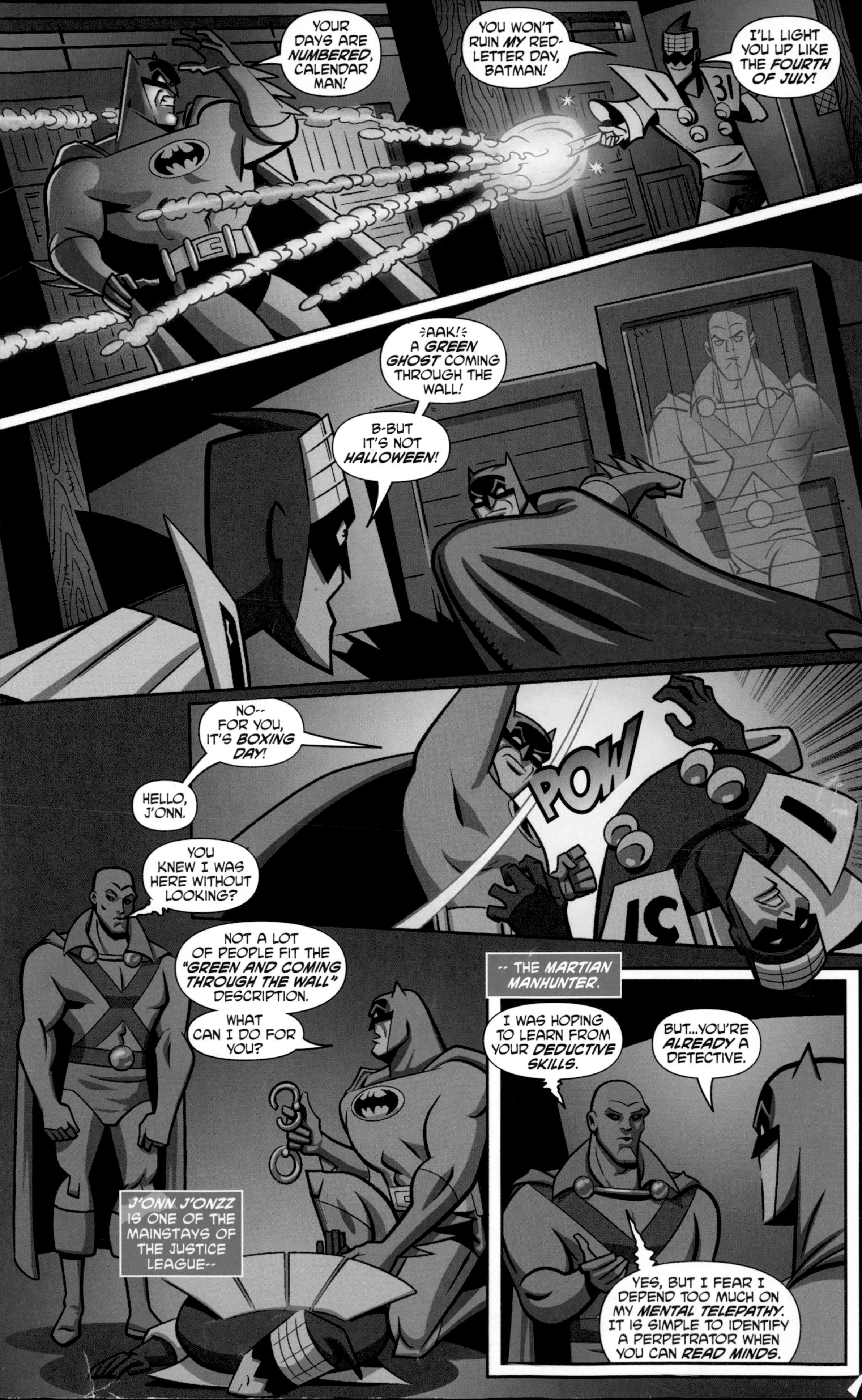

YOUR DAYS ARE *NUMBERED*, CALENDAR MAN!
YOU WON'T RUIN *MY* RED-LETTER DAY, BATMAN!
I'LL LIGHT YOU UP LIKE THE *FOURTH OF JULY!*
AAK! A *GREEN GHOST* COMING THROUGH THE WALL!
B-BUT IT'S NOT *HALLOWEEN!*
NO-- FOR YOU, IT'S *BOXING DAY!*
POW
HELLO, J'ONN.
YOU KNEW I WAS HERE WITHOUT LOOKING?
NOT A LOT OF PEOPLE FIT THE *"GREEN AND COMING THROUGH THE WALL"* DESCRIPTION.
WHAT CAN I DO FOR YOU?
J'ONN J'ONZZ IS ONE OF THE MAINSTAYS OF THE JUSTICE LEAGUE--
-- THE *MARTIAN MANHUNTER*.
I WAS HOPING TO LEARN FROM YOUR *DEDUCTIVE SKILLS*.
BUT...YOU'RE *ALREADY* A DETECTIVE.
YES, BUT I FEAR I DEPEND TOO MUCH ON MY *MENTAL TELEPATHY*. IT IS SIMPLE TO IDENTIFY A PERPETRATOR WHEN YOU CAN *READ MINDS*.

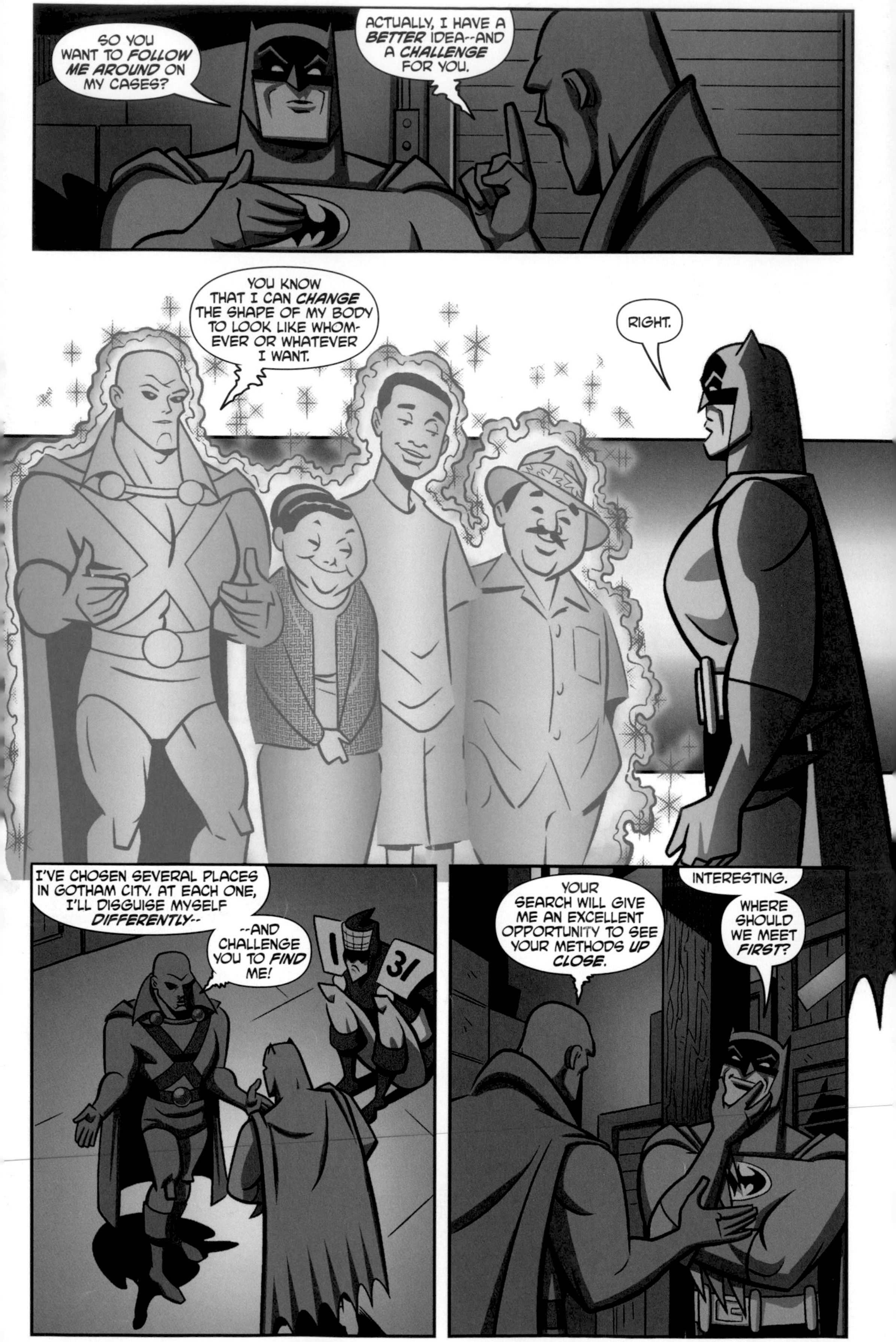
SO YOU WANT TO *FOLLOW ME AROUND* ON MY CASES?
ACTUALLY, I HAVE A *BETTER* IDEA--AND A *CHALLENGE* FOR YOU.
YOU KNOW THAT I CAN *CHANGE* THE SHAPE OF MY BODY TO LOOK LIKE WHOMEVER OR WHATEVER I WANT.
RIGHT.
I'VE CHOSEN SEVERAL PLACES IN GOTHAM CITY. AT EACH ONE, I'LL DISGUISE MYSELF *DIFFERENTLY*--
--AND CHALLENGE YOU TO *FIND* ME!
31
YOUR SEARCH WILL GIVE ME AN EXCELLENT OPPORTUNITY TO SEE YOUR METHODS *UP CLOSE*.
INTERESTING.
WHERE SHOULD WE MEET *FIRST?*

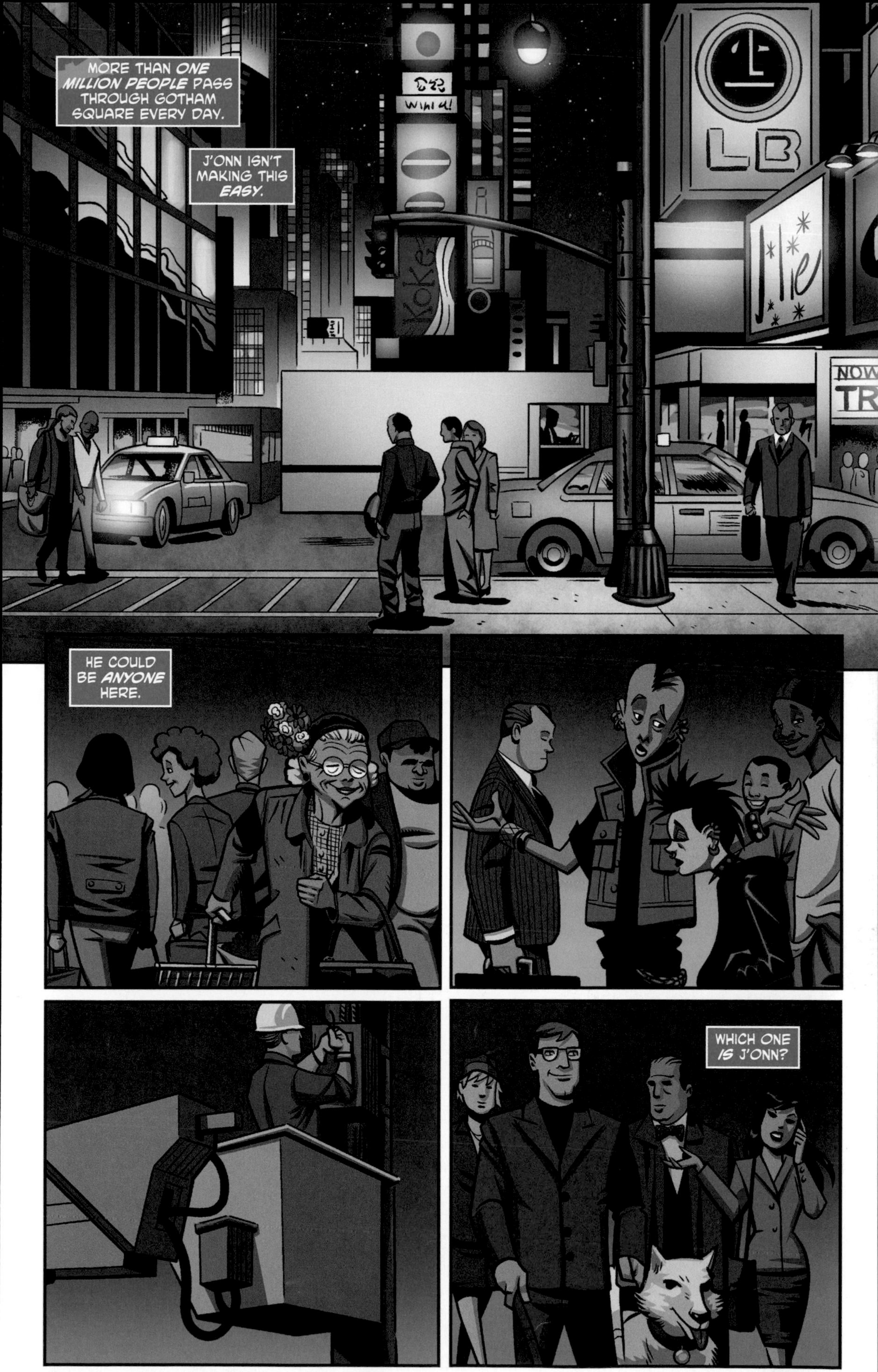
MORE THAN ONE MILLION PEOPLE PASS THROUGH GOTHAM SQUARE EVERY DAY.
J'ONN ISN'T MAKING THIS EASY.
HE COULD BE ANYONE HERE.
WHICH ONE IS J'ONN?

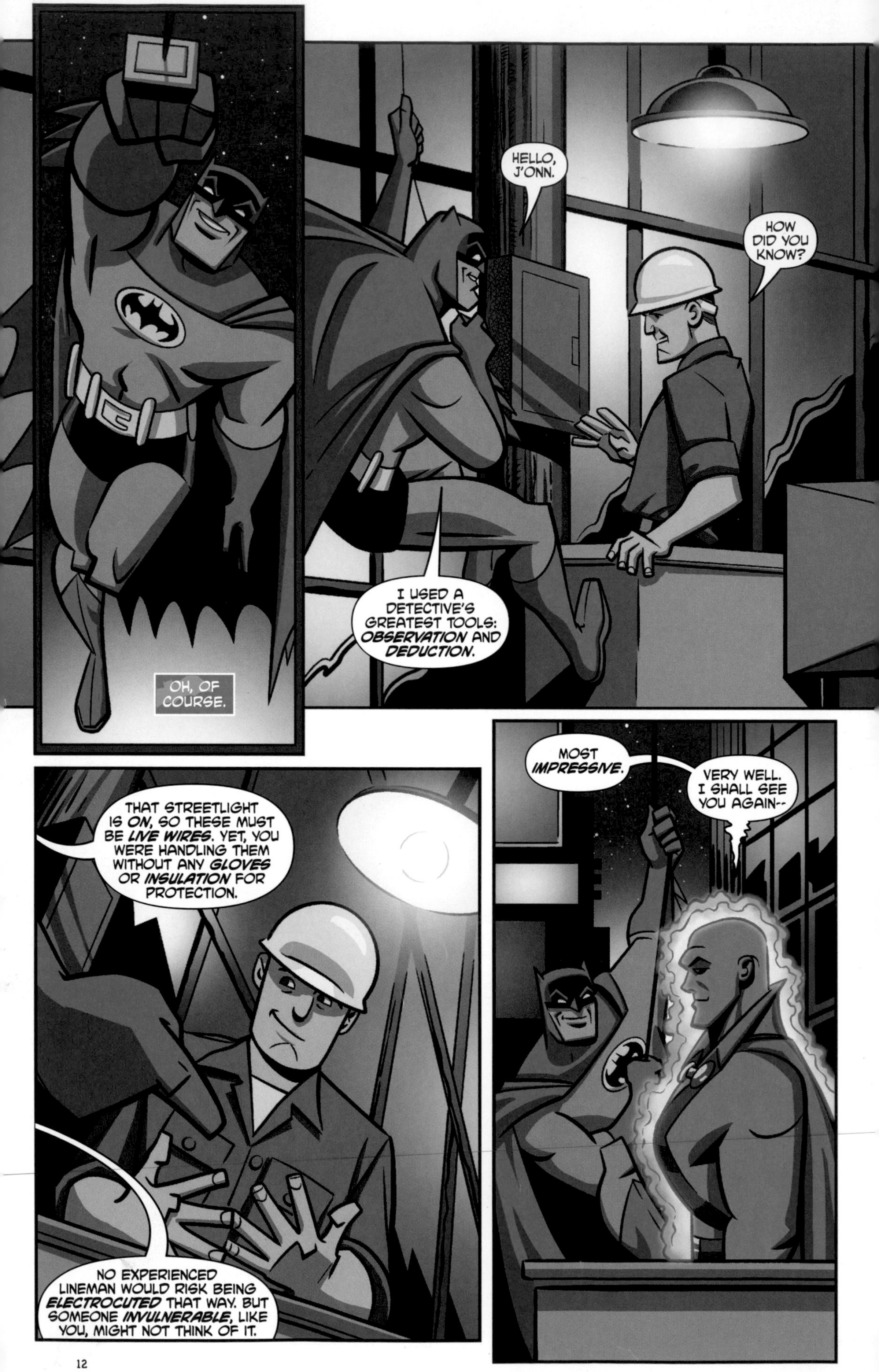
HELLO, J'ONN.
HOW DID YOU KNOW?
I USED A DETECTIVE'S GREATEST TOOLS: *OBSERVATION* AND *DEDUCTION*.
OH, OF COURSE.
THAT STREETLIGHT IS *ON*, SO THESE MUST BE *LIVE WIRES*. YET, YOU WERE HANDLING THEM WITHOUT ANY *GLOVES* OR *INSULATION* FOR PROTECTION.
NO EXPERIENCED LINEMAN WOULD RISK BEING *ELECTROCUTED* THAT WAY. BUT SOMEONE *INVULNERABLE*, LIKE YOU, MIGHT NOT THINK OF IT.
MOST *IMPRESSIVE*.
VERY WELL. I SHALL SEE YOU AGAIN--

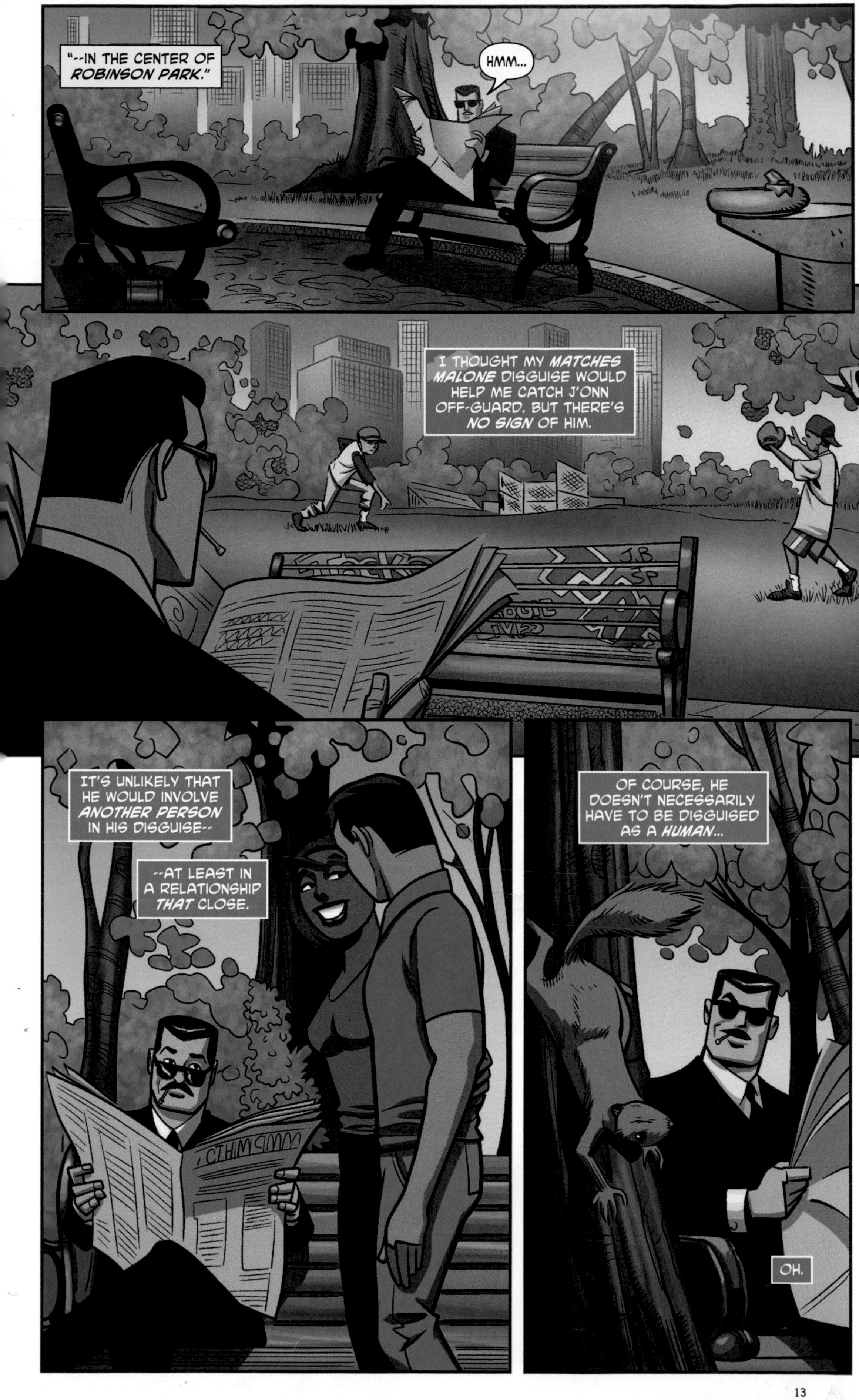
"--IN THE CENTER OF ROBINSON PARK."
HMM...
I THOUGHT MY MATCHES MALONE DISGUISE WOULD HELP ME CATCH J'ONN OFF-GUARD. BUT THERE'S NO SIGN OF HIM.
IT'S UNLIKELY THAT HE WOULD INVOLVE ANOTHER PERSON IN HIS DISGUISE--
--AT LEAST IN A RELATIONSHIP THAT CLOSE.
OF COURSE, HE DOESN'T NECESSARILY HAVE TO BE DISGUISED AS A HUMAN...
OH.

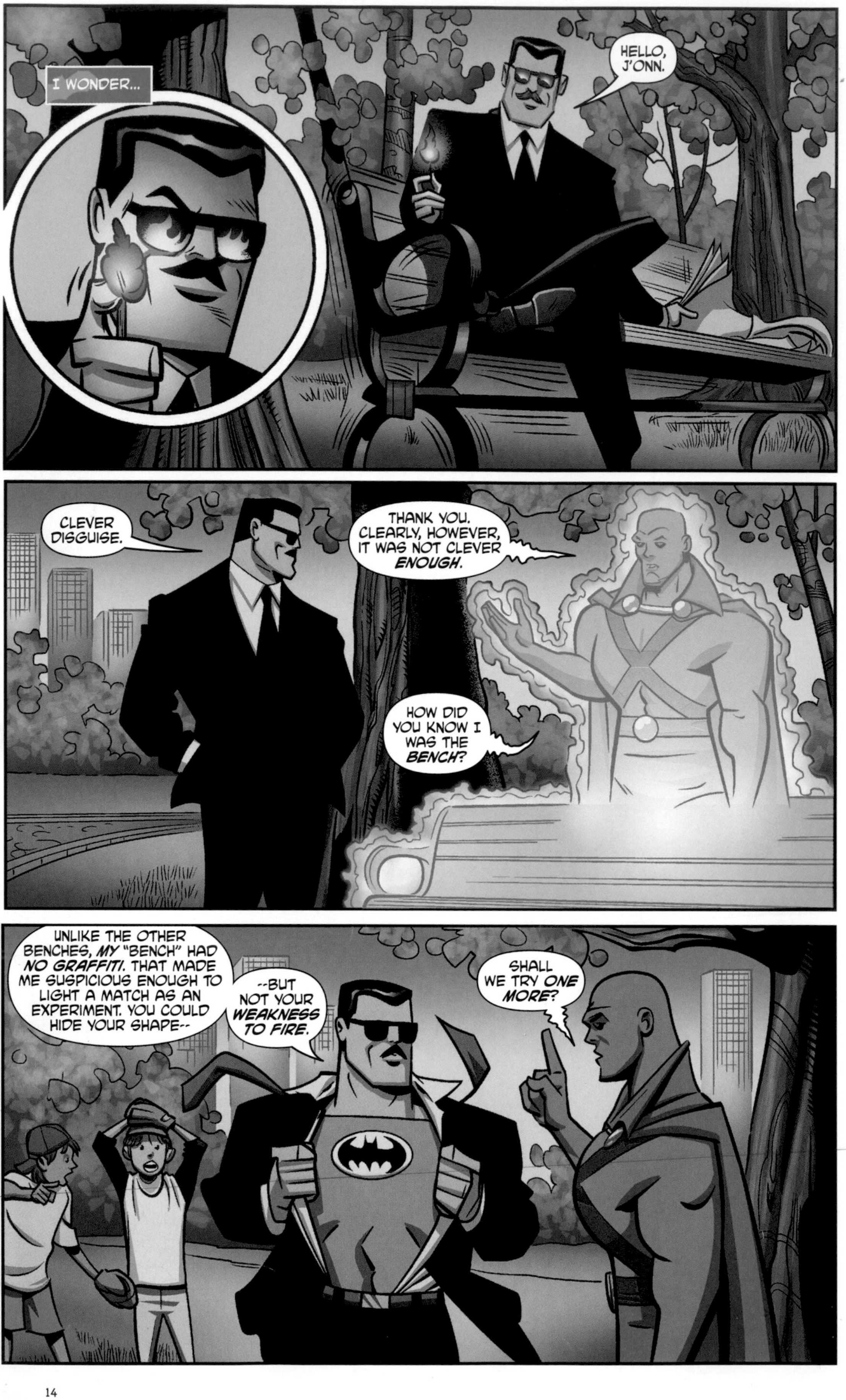
I WONDER...
HELLO, J'ONN.
CLEVER DISGUISE.
THANK YOU. CLEARLY, HOWEVER, IT WAS NOT CLEVER *ENOUGH*.
HOW DID YOU KNOW I WAS THE *BENCH*?
UNLIKE THE OTHER BENCHES, *MY* "BENCH" HAD *NO GRAFFITI*. THAT MADE ME SUSPICIOUS ENOUGH TO LIGHT A MATCH AS AN EXPERIMENT. YOU COULD HIDE YOUR SHAPE--
--BUT NOT YOUR *WEAKNESS TO FIRE*.
SHALL WE TRY *ONE MORE*?

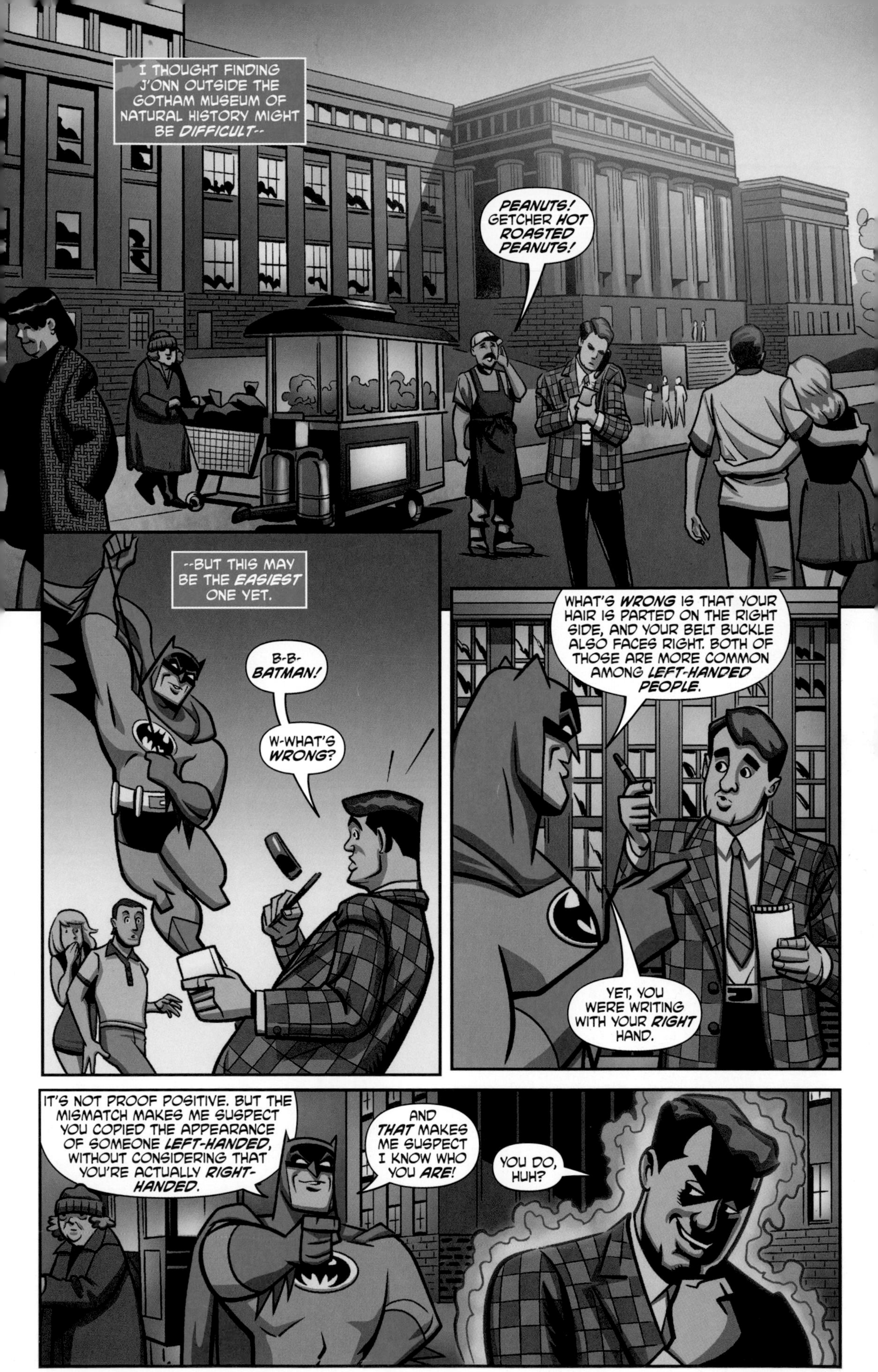

I THOUGHT FINDING J'ONN OUTSIDE THE GOTHAM MUSEUM OF NATURAL HISTORY MIGHT BE DIFFICULT--
PEANUTS! GETCHER HOT ROASTED PEANUTS!
--BUT THIS MAY BE THE EASIEST ONE YET.
B-B-BATMAN!
W-WHAT'S WRONG?
WHAT'S WRONG IS THAT YOUR HAIR IS PARTED ON THE RIGHT SIDE, AND YOUR BELT BUCKLE ALSO FACES RIGHT. BOTH OF THOSE ARE MORE COMMON AMONG LEFT-HANDED PEOPLE.
YET, YOU WERE WRITING WITH YOUR RIGHT HAND.
IT'S NOT PROOF POSITIVE. BUT THE MISMATCH MAKES ME SUSPECT YOU COPIED THE APPEARANCE OF SOMEONE LEFT-HANDED, WITHOUT CONSIDERING THAT YOU'RE ACTUALLY RIGHT-HANDED.
AND THAT MAKES ME SUSPECT I KNOW WHO YOU ARE!
YOU DO, HUH?

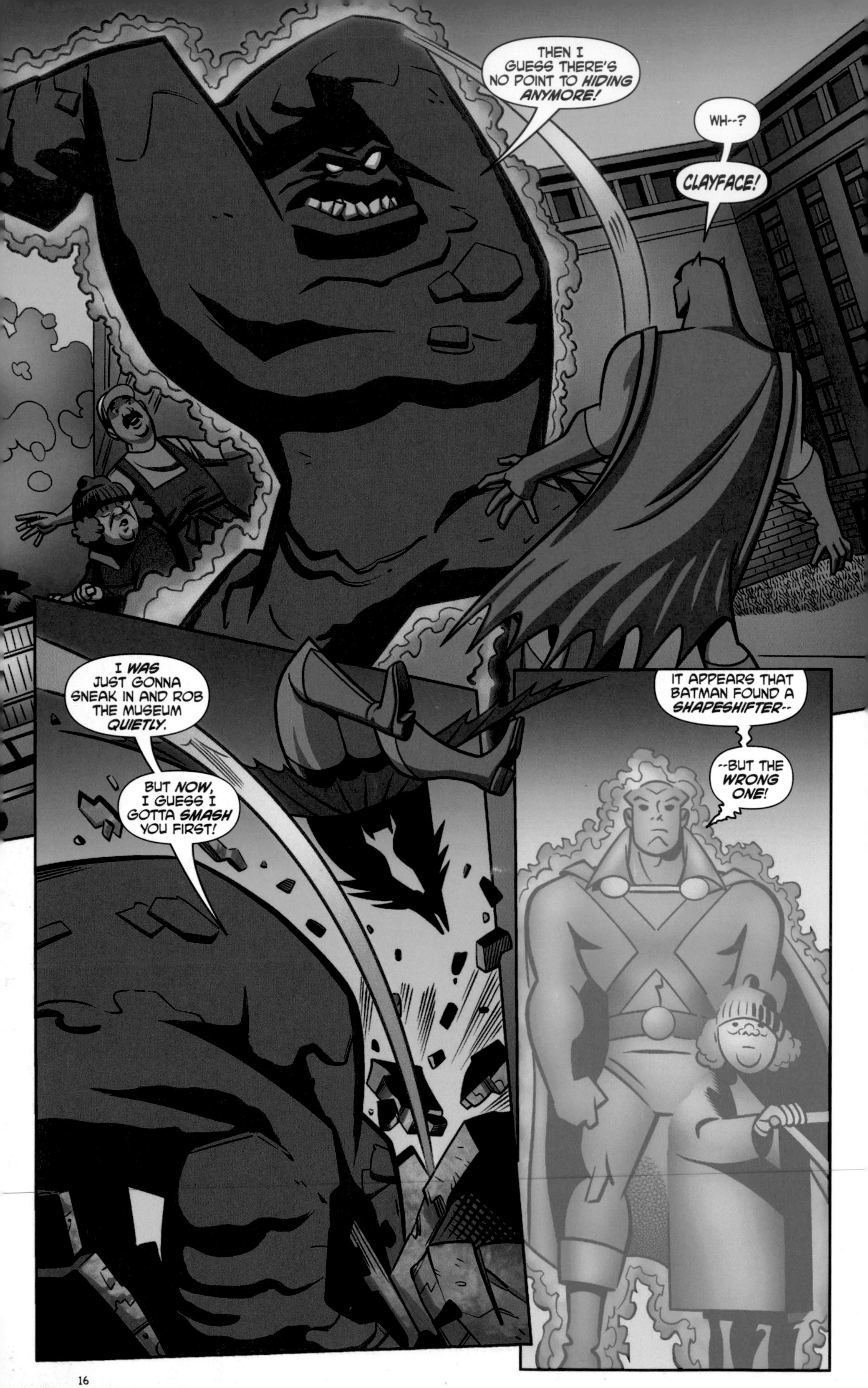
THEN I GUESS THERE'S NO POINT TO HIDING ANYMORE!
WH--?
CLAYFACE!
I WAS JUST GONNA SNEAK IN AND ROB THE MUSEUM QUIETLY.
BUT NOW, I GUESS I GOTTA SMASH YOU FIRST!
IT APPEARS THAT BATMAN FOUND A SHAPESHIFTER--
--BUT THE WRONG ONE!

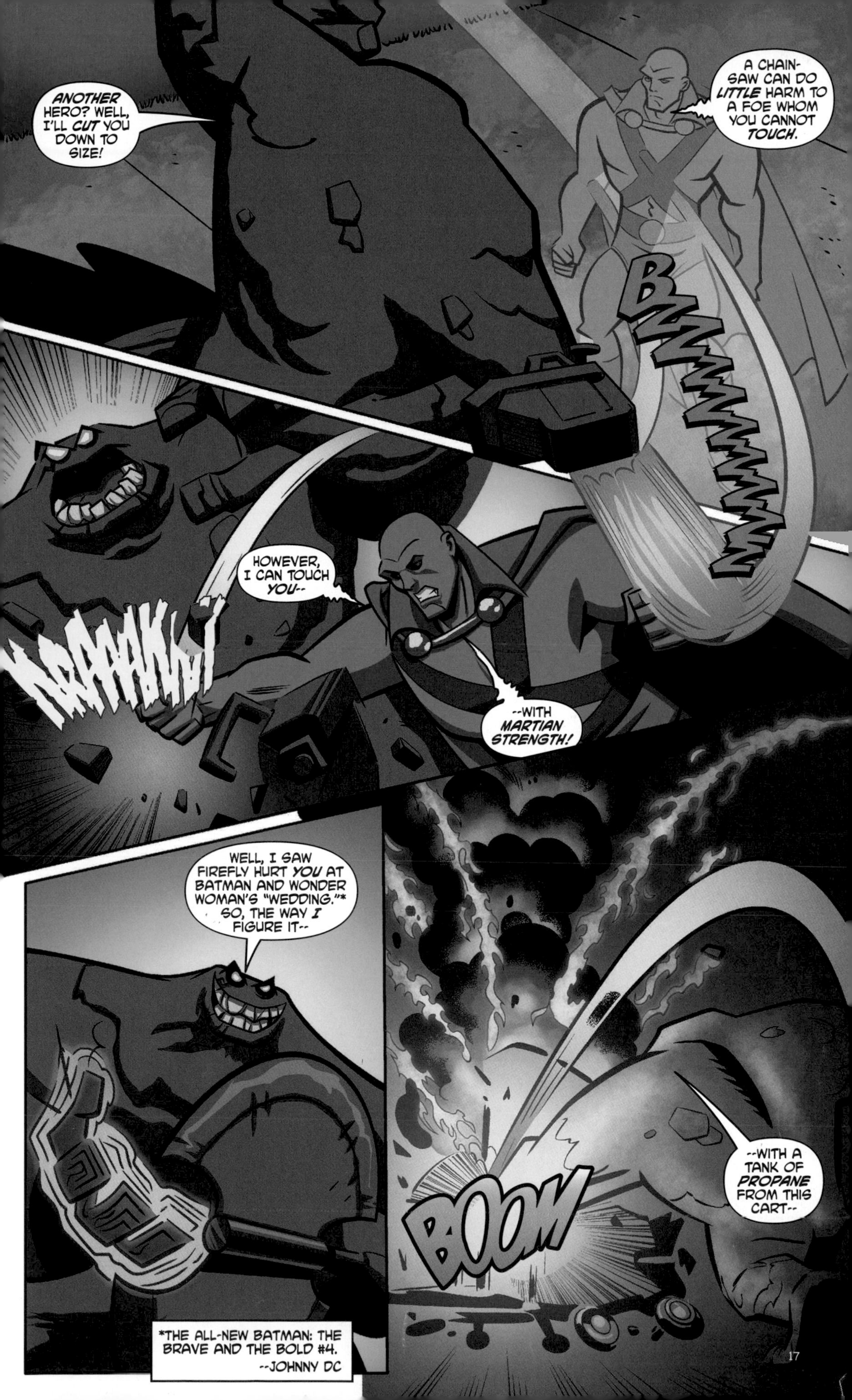
ANOTHER HERO? WELL, I'LL CUT YOU DOWN TO SIZE!
A CHAIN-SAW CAN DO LITTLE HARM TO A FOE WHOM YOU CANNOT TOUCH.
BZZZMMMMMMM
HOWEVER, I CAN TOUCH YOU--
KRAKK!
--WITH MARTIAN STRENGTH!
WELL, I SAW FIREFLY HURT YOU AT BATMAN AND WONDER WOMAN'S "WEDDING."* SO, THE WAY I FIGURE IT--
*THE ALL-NEW BATMAN: THE BRAVE AND THE BOLD #4. --JOHNNY DC
BOOM
--WITH A TANK OF PROPANE FROM THIS CART--

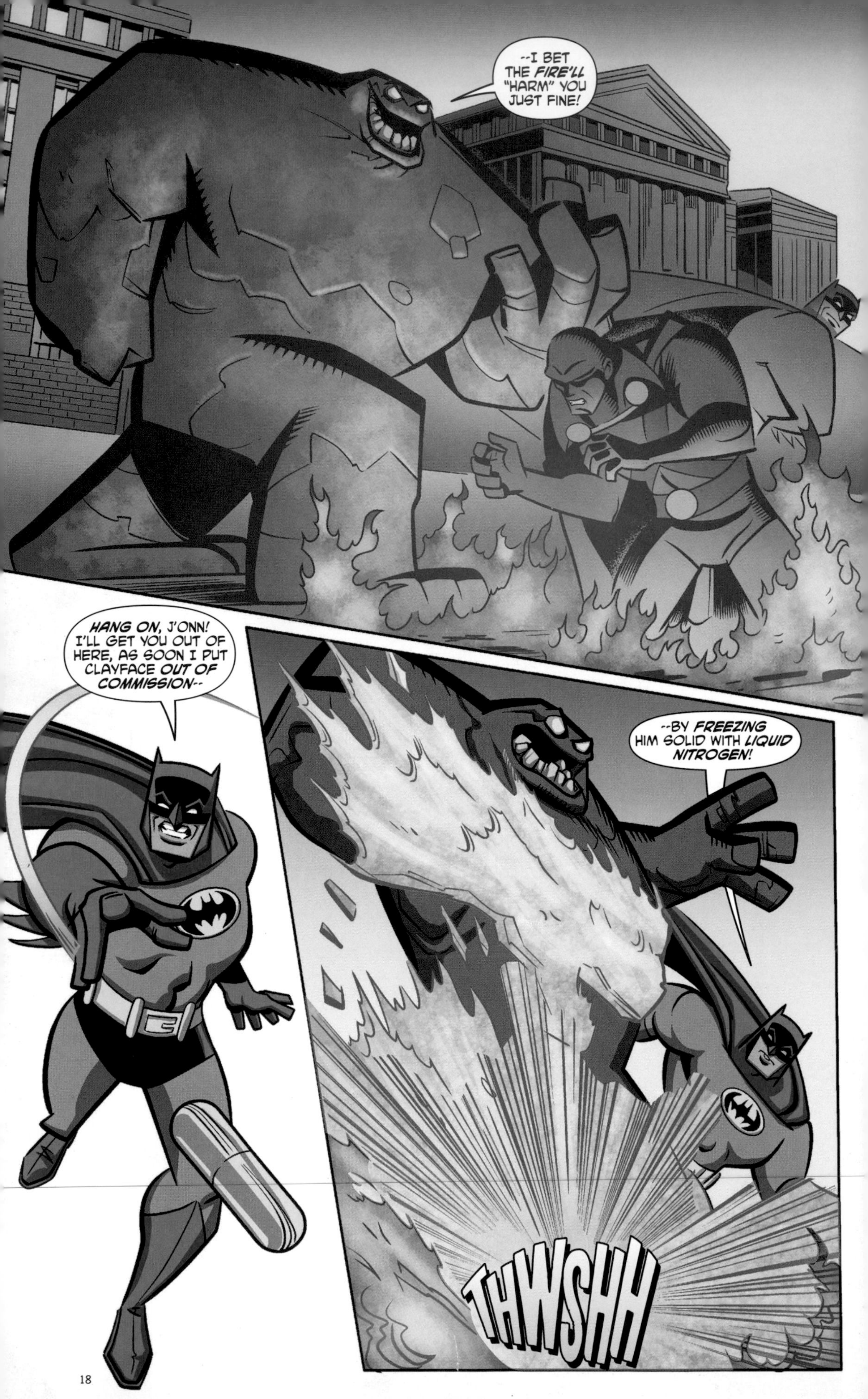
--I BET THE FIRE'LL "HARM" YOU JUST FINE!
HANG ON, J'ONN! I'LL GET YOU OUT OF HERE, AS SOON I PUT CLAYFACE OUT OF COMMISSION--
--BY FREEZING HIM SOLID WITH LIQUID NITROGEN!
THWSHH

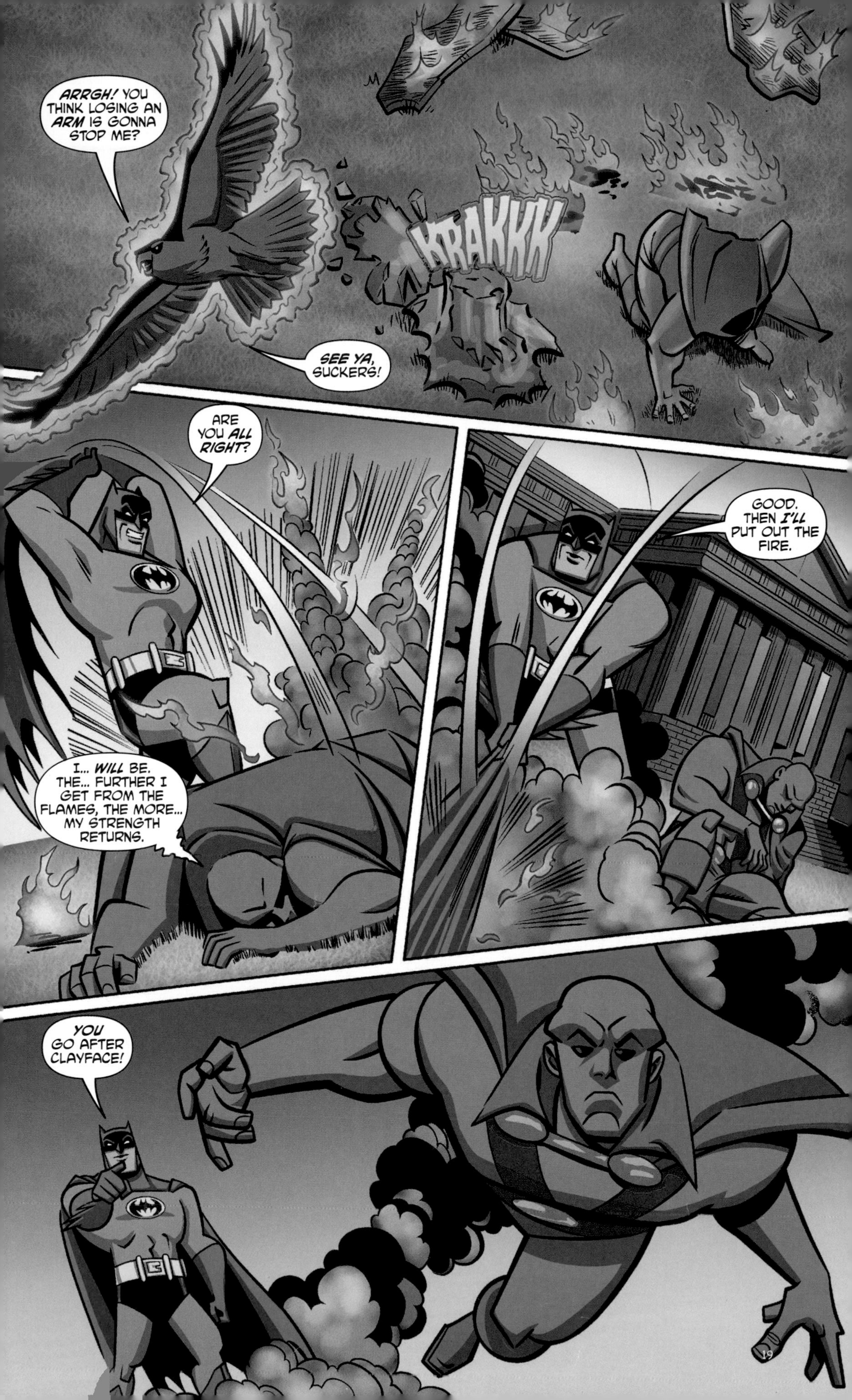

ARRGH! YOU THINK LOSING AN ARM IS GONNA STOP ME?
KRAKKK
SEE YA, SUCKERS!
ARE YOU ALL RIGHT?
I... WILL BE. THE... FURTHER I GET FROM THE FLAMES, THE MORE... MY STRENGTH RETURNS.
GOOD. THEN I'LL PUT OUT THE FIRE.
YOU GO AFTER CLAYFACE!

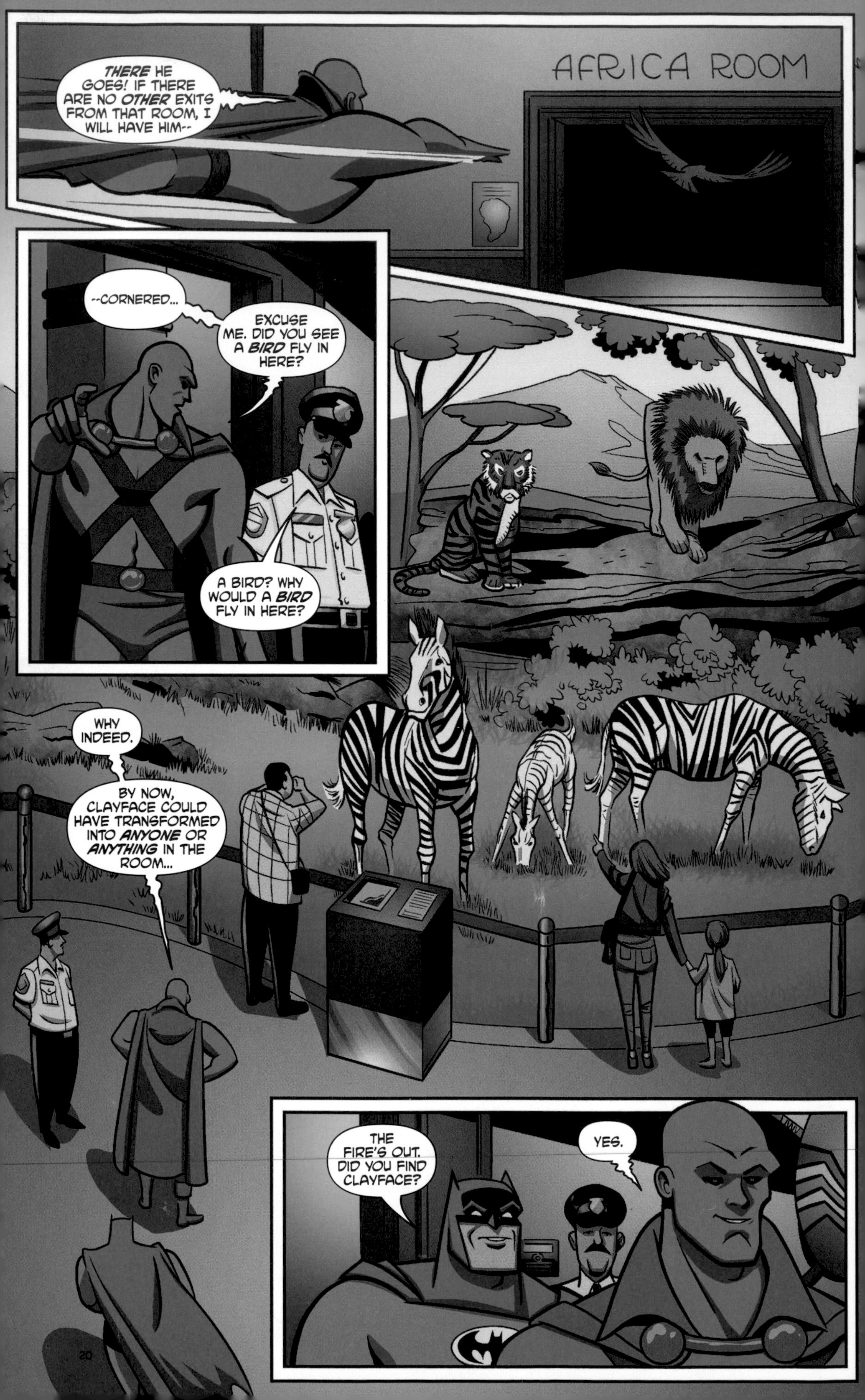

THERE HE GOES! IF THERE ARE NO OTHER EXITS FROM THAT ROOM, I WILL HAVE HIM--
AFRICA ROOM
--CORNERED...
EXCUSE ME. DID YOU SEE A BIRD FLY IN HERE?
A BIRD? WHY WOULD A BIRD FLY IN HERE?
WHY INDEED.
BY NOW, CLAYFACE COULD HAVE TRANSFORMED INTO ANYONE OR ANYTHING IN THE ROOM...
THE FIRE'S OUT. DID YOU FIND CLAYFACE?
YES.

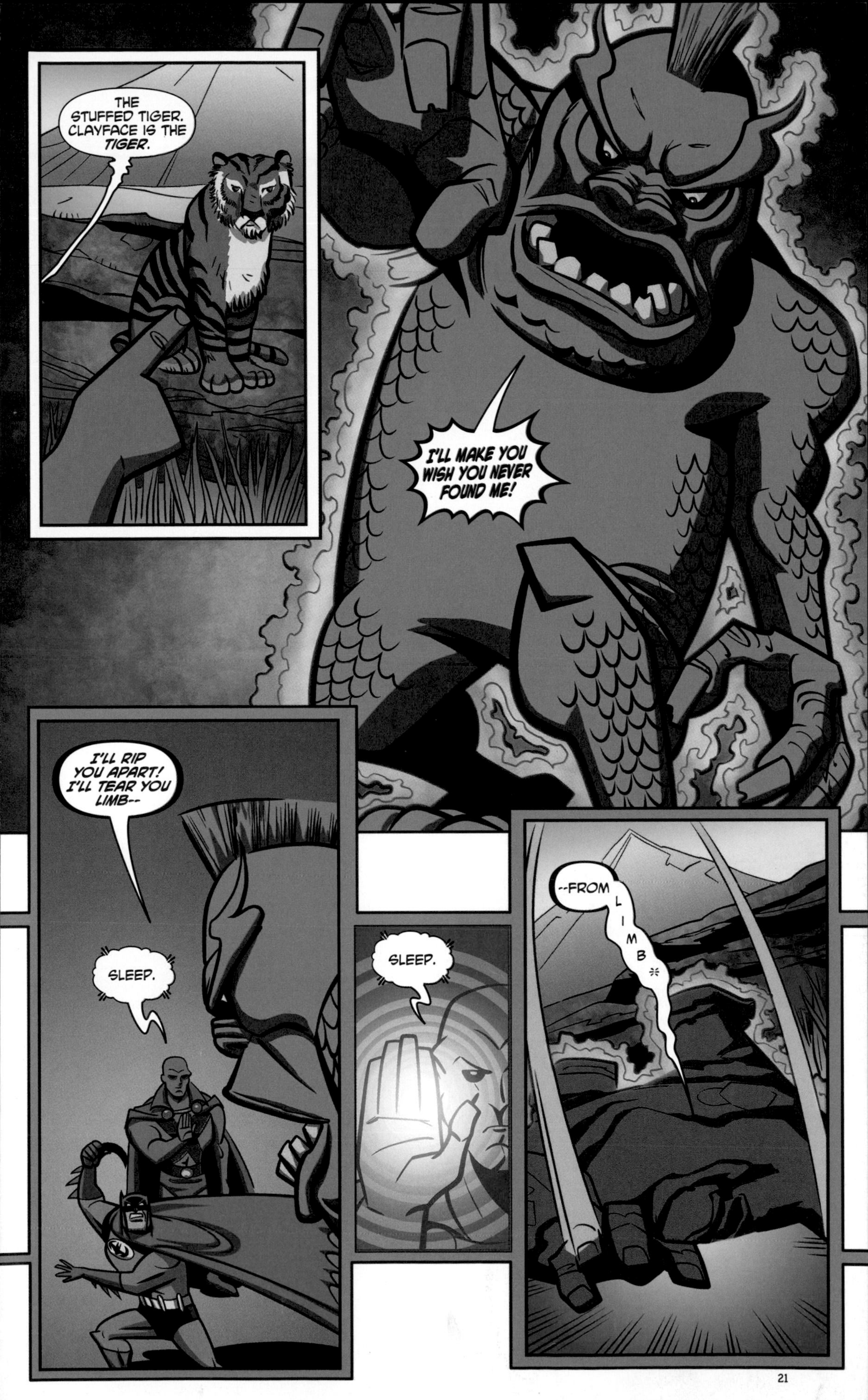
THE STUFFED TIGER. CLAYFACE IS THE *TIGER*.
I'LL MAKE YOU WISH YOU NEVER FOUND ME!
I'LL RIP YOU APART! I'LL TEAR YOU LIMB--
SLEEP.
SLEEP.
--FROM LIMB!

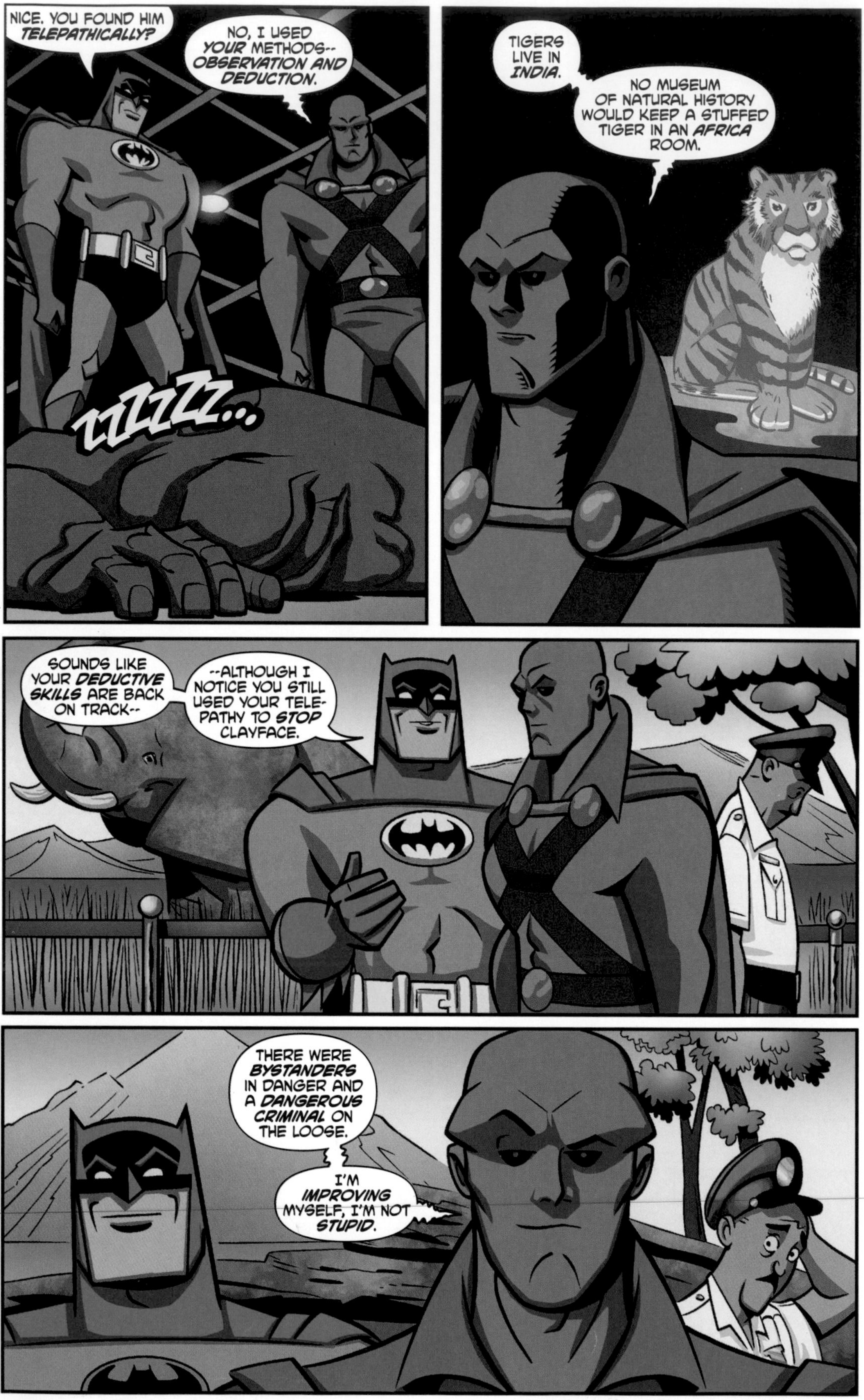

NICE. YOU FOUND HIM TELEPATHICALLY?
NO, I USED YOUR METHODS-- OBSERVATION AND DEDUCTION.
ZZZZZZ...
TIGERS LIVE IN INDIA.
NO MUSEUM OF NATURAL HISTORY WOULD KEEP A STUFFED TIGER IN AN AFRICA ROOM.
SOUNDS LIKE YOUR DEDUCTIVE SKILLS ARE BACK ON TRACK--
--ALTHOUGH I NOTICE YOU STILL USED YOUR TELEPATHY TO STOP CLAYFACE.
THERE WERE BYSTANDERS IN DANGER AND A DANGEROUS CRIMINAL ON THE LOOSE.
I'M IMPROVING MYSELF, I'M NOT STUPID.

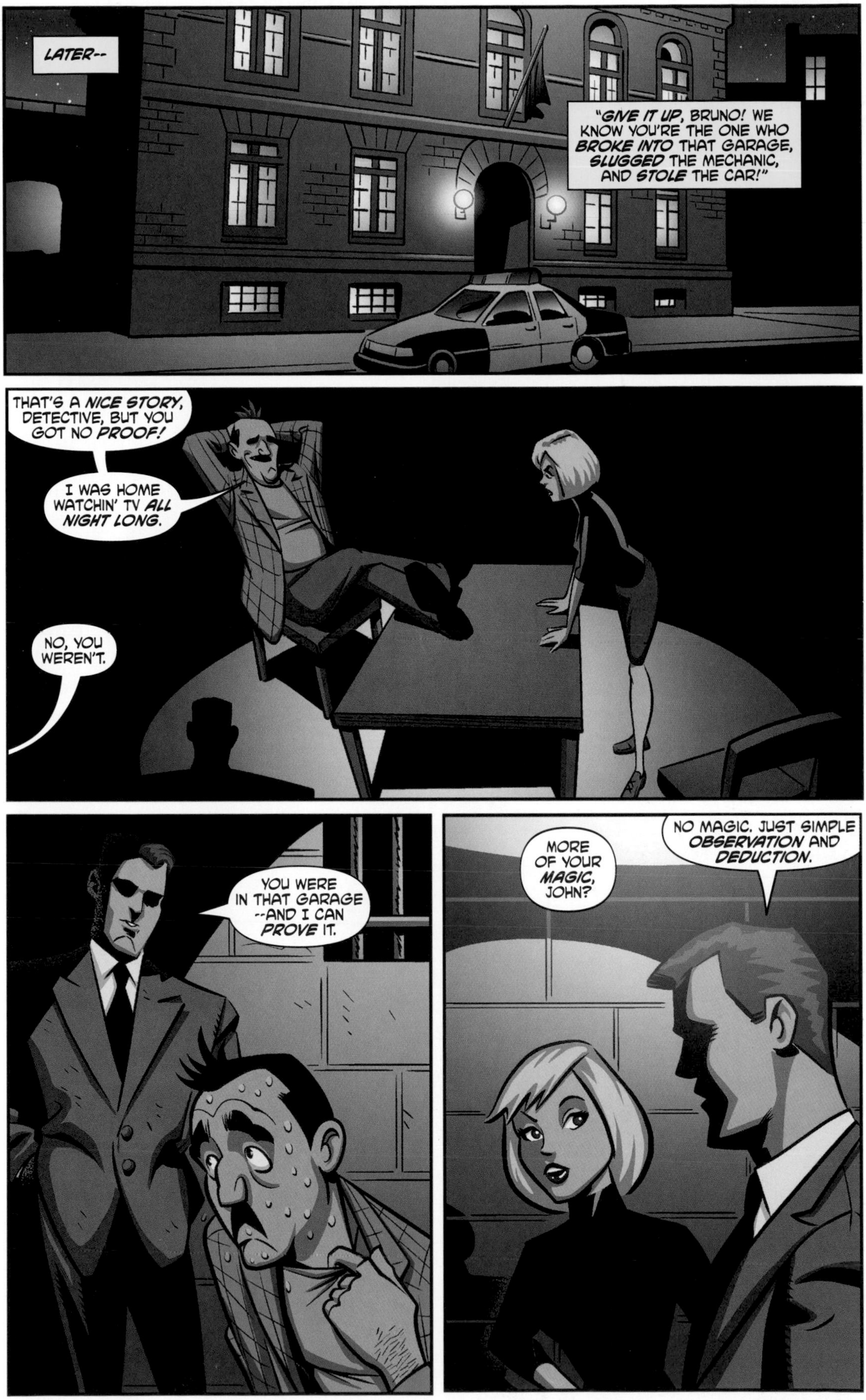
LATER--
"GIVE IT UP, BRUNO! WE KNOW YOU'RE THE ONE WHO BROKE INTO THAT GARAGE, SLUGGED THE MECHANIC, AND STOLE THE CAR!"
THAT'S A NICE STORY, DETECTIVE, BUT YOU GOT NO PROOF!
I WAS HOME WATCHIN' TV ALL NIGHT LONG.
NO, YOU WEREN'T.
YOU WERE IN THAT GARAGE --AND I CAN PROVE IT.
MORE OF YOUR MAGIC, JOHN?
NO MAGIC. JUST SIMPLE OBSERVATION AND DEDUCTION.

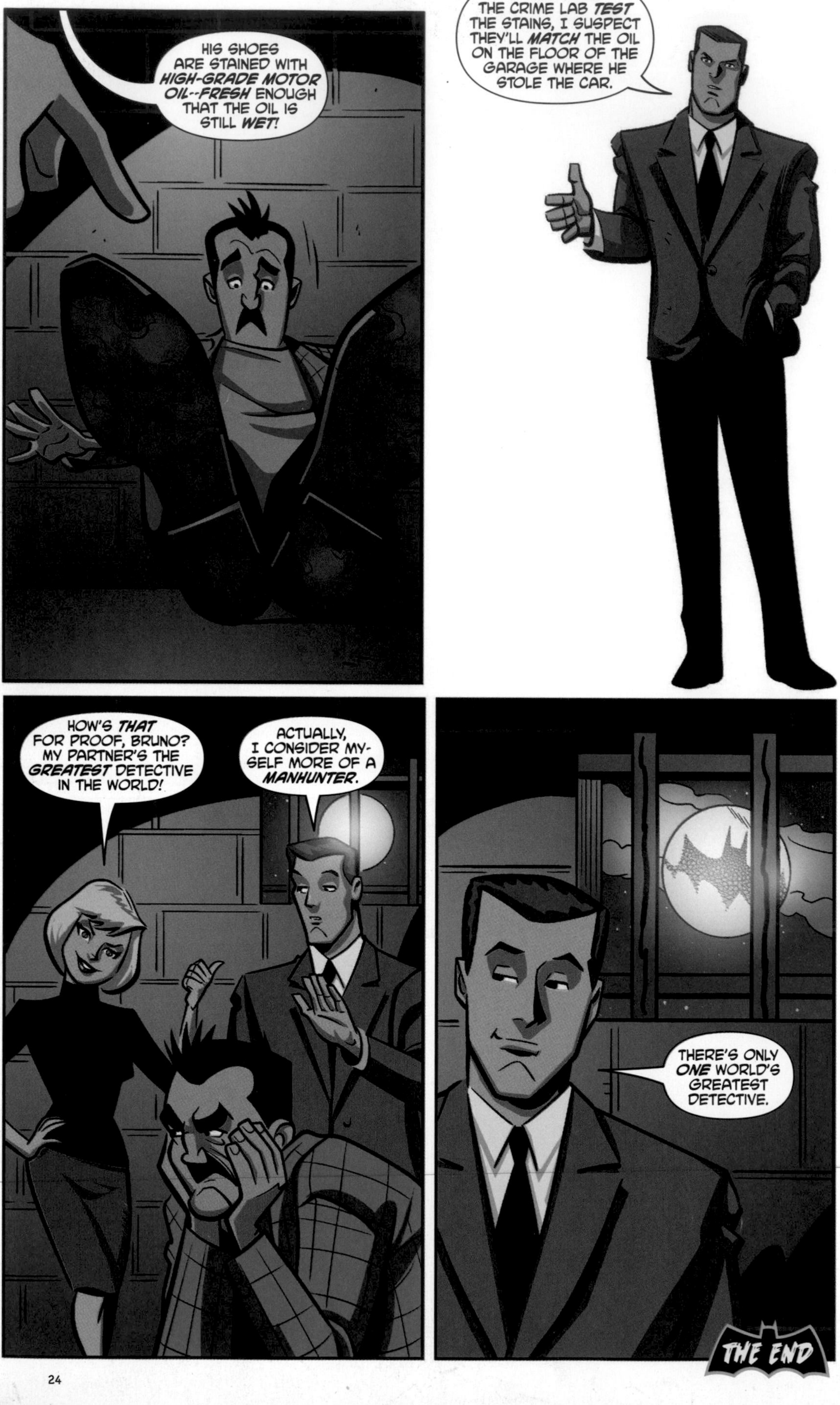
HIS SHOES ARE STAINED WITH HIGH-GRADE MOTOR OIL--FRESH ENOUGH THAT THE OIL IS STILL WET!
IF YOU HAVE THE CRIME LAB TEST THE STAINS, I SUSPECT THEY'LL MATCH THE OIL ON THE FLOOR OF THE GARAGE WHERE HE STOLE THE CAR.
HOW'S THAT FOR PROOF, BRUNO? MY PARTNER'S THE GREATEST DETECTIVE IN THE WORLD!
ACTUALLY, I CONSIDER MY-SELF MORE OF A MANHUNTER.
THERE'S ONLY ONE WORLD'S GREATEST DETECTIVE.
THE END

CREATORS

SHOLLY FISCH
WRITER

Bitten by a radioactive typewriter, Sholly Fisch has spent the wee hours writing books, comics, TV scripts, and online material for over 25 years. His comic book credits include more than 200 stories and features about characters such as Batman, Superman, Bugs Bunny, Daffy Duck, Spider-Man, and Ben 10. Currently, he writes stories for Action Comics every month, plus stories for Looney Tunes and Scooby-Doo. By day, Sholly is a mild-mannered developmental psychologist who helps to create educational TV shows, websites, and other media for kids.

RICK BURCHETT
PENCILLER

Rick Burchett has worked as a comics artist for over 25 years. He has received the comics industry's Eisner Award three times, Spain's Haxtur Award, and he has been nominated for England's Eagle Award. Rick lives with his wife and two sons near St. Louis, Missouri.

DAN DAVIS
INKER

Dan Davis has illustrated the Garfield comic series as well as books for Warner Bros. and DC Comics. He has brought a variety of comic book characters to life, including Batman and the rest of the Super Friends! In 2012, Dan was nominated for an Eisner Award for the Batman: The Brave and the Bold series. He currently resides in Gotham City.

GLOSSARY

bystander [BYE·stan·dur]--someone who is nearby when something happens to someone else

deduction [di·DUHK·shuhn]--the act of figuring something out through using little details and pieces of information

description [di·SKRIP·shuhn]--a statement that tells how something looks

disguise [dis·GIZE]--to hide something, especially by changing the way it looks

insulation [IN·suh·LAY·shuhn]--material that covers something to stop heat, electricity, or sound from escaping

invulnerable [in·VUHL·ner·uh·buhl]--unable to be hurt or damaged

observation [ohb·zur·VAY·shuhn]--the act of closely and carefully watching something and looking at small details

perpetrator [PUR·pi·tray·ter]--a person who commits a crime or evil act

suspicious [suh·SPISH·uhss]--feeling like something is wrong or bad, even though there's no proof

telepathy [tuh·LEP·uh·thee]--the ability to read a person's mind and communicate without words or signs

warrant [WAWR·uhnt]--an official document that gives a person the right to do something, like make an arrest or search a house

VISUAL QUESTIONS & PROMPTS

1. Why do you think the artists chose to make the Martian Manhunter's word balloon tails jagged?

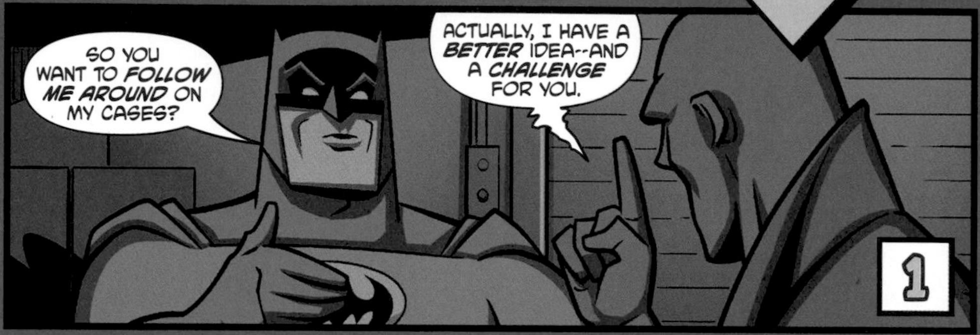
SO YOU WANT TO *FOLLOW ME AROUND* ON MY CASES?
ACTUALLY, I HAVE A *BETTER* IDEA--AND A *CHALLENGE* FOR YOU.
1

2. If you had to guess that someone in this picture was J'onn, who would you guess and why?

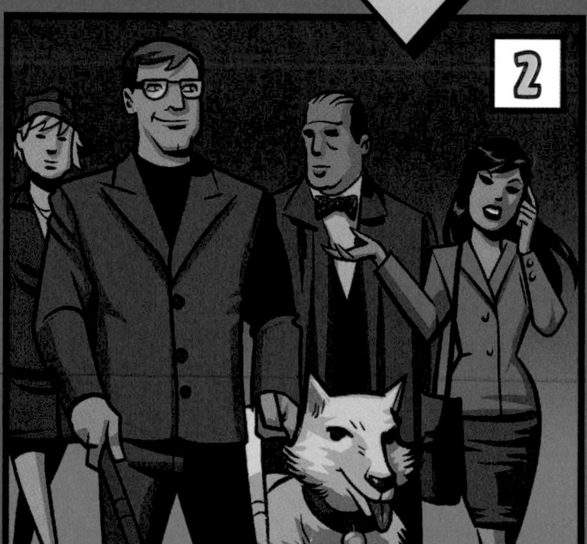
2

3. How does the art help us predict that this man is not who Batman expects him to be? What clues do the artists give us?

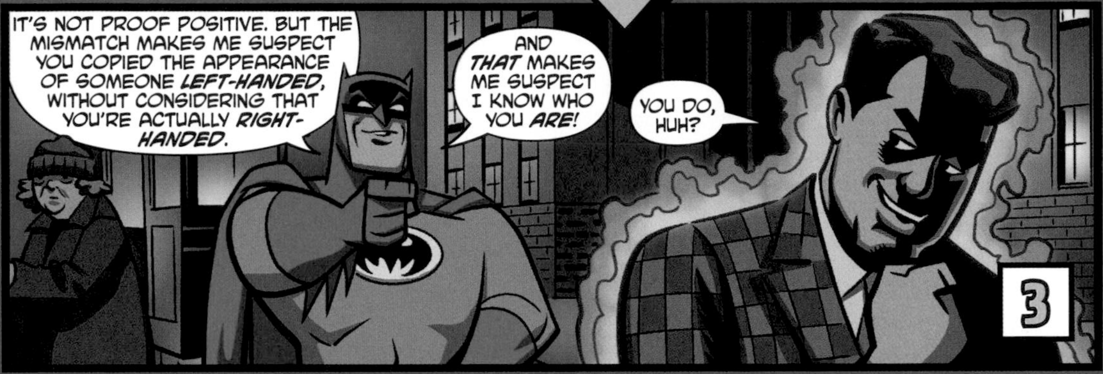
IT'S NOT PROOF POSITIVE. BUT THE MISMATCH MAKES ME SUSPECT YOU COPIED THE APPEARANCE OF SOMEONE *LEFT-HANDED*, WITHOUT CONSIDERING THAT YOU'RE ACTUALLY *RIGHT-HANDED*.
AND *THAT* MAKES ME SUSPECT I KNOW WHO YOU *ARE*!
YOU DO, HUH?
3

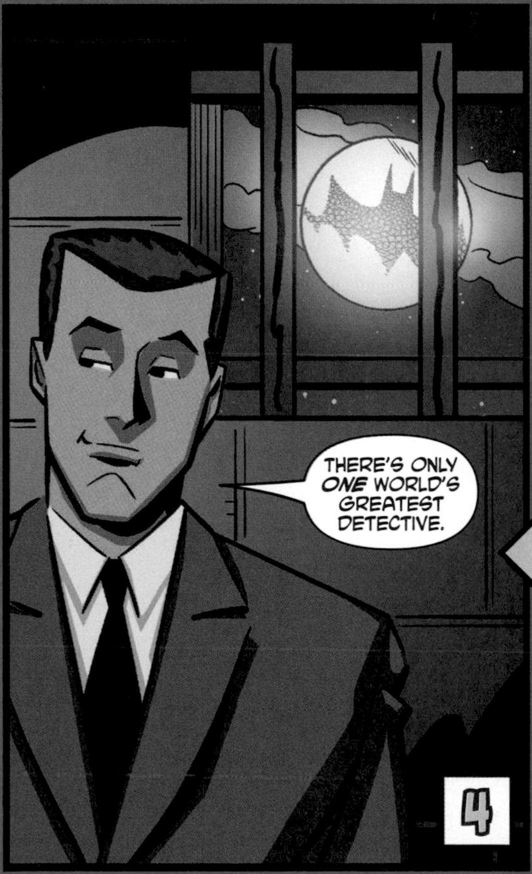
THERE'S ONLY *ONE* WORLD'S GREATEST DETECTIVE.
4

4. Who is J'onn talking about in this panel? How do you know?

READ THEM ALL!

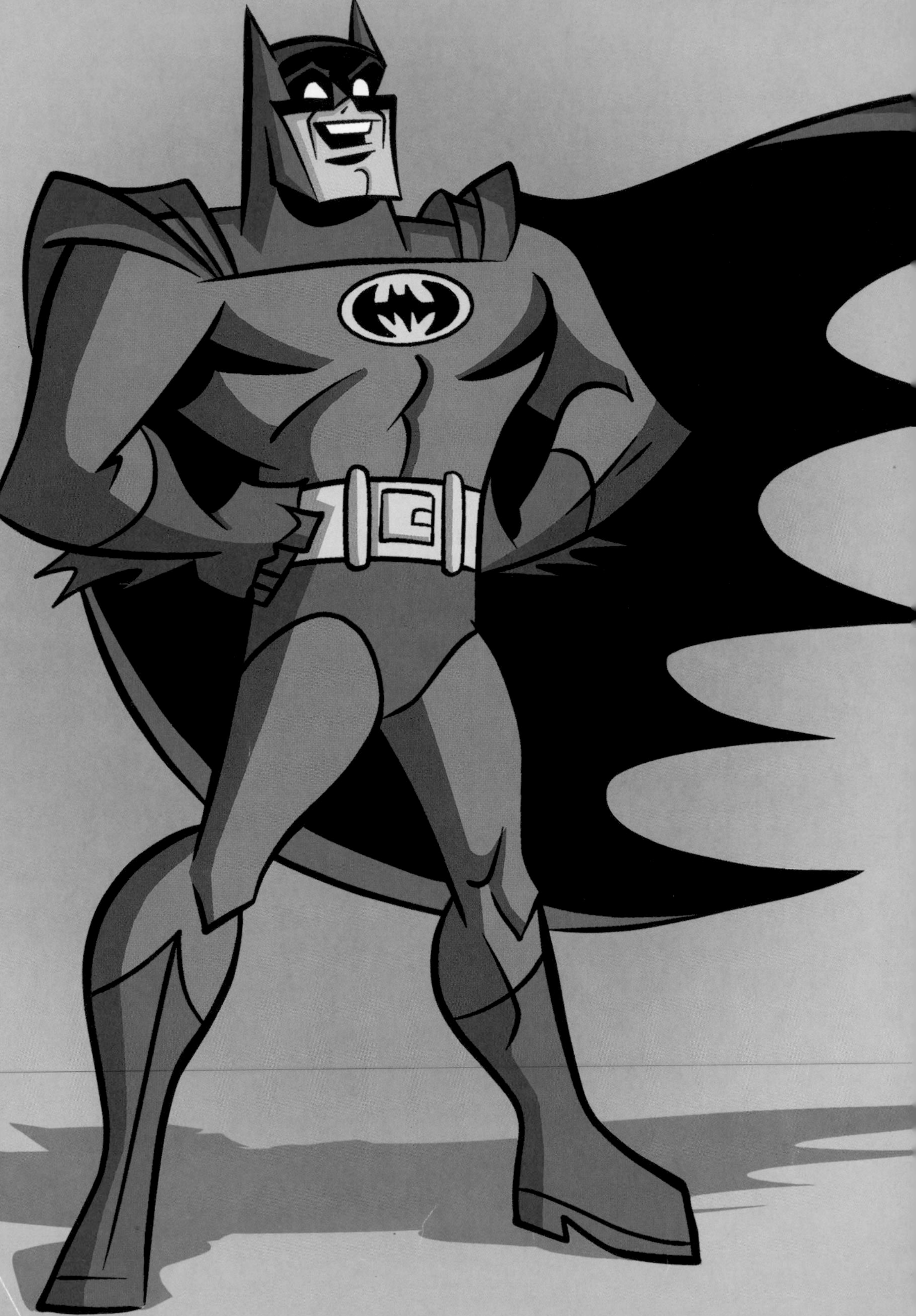

THE ALL NEW!

BATMAN

THE BRAVE AND THE BOLD

THE ALL NEW!
BATMAN
THE BRAVE AND THE BOLD
BOTTLE OF THE PLANETS
FISCH
BURCHETT
DAVIS

THE ALL NEW!
BATMAN
THE BRAVE AND THE BOLD
THAT HOLIDAY FEELING
FISCH
BURCHETT
DAVIS

THE ALL NEW!
BATMAN
THE BRAVE AND THE BOLD
THROUGH THE LOOKING GLASS
FISCH
BURCHETT
DAVIS

THE ALL NEW!
BATMAN
THE BRAVE AND THE BOLD
FISCH
BURCHETT
DAVIS
THE BRIDE AND THE BOLD

THE ALL NEW!
BATMAN
THE BRAVE AND THE BOLD
FISCH
BURCHETT
DAVIS
MANHANDLED BY MANHUNTERS!

THE ALL NEW!
BATMAN
THE BRAVE AND THE BOLD
FISCH
BURCHETT
DAVIS
CLOBBERED BY CLAYFACE!

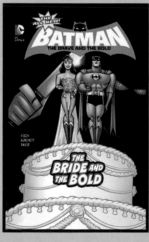

THE ALL NEW!

BATMAN

THE BRAVE AND THE BOLD

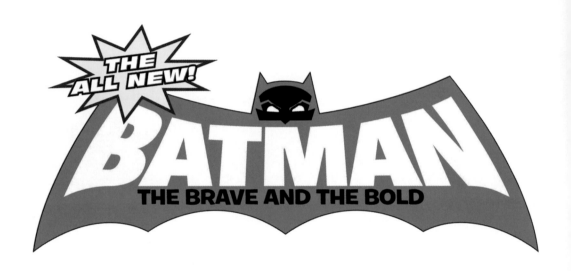